MARIE

LAURA E. RICHARDS

MARIE

CHAPTER I

MARIE.

Marie was tired. She had been walking nearly the whole day, and now the sun was low in the west, and long level rays of yellow light were spreading over the country, striking the windows of a farmhouse here and there into sudden flame, or resting more softly on tree-tops and hanging slopes. They were like fiddle-bows, Marie thought; and at the thought she held closer something that she carried in her arms, and murmured over it a little, as a mother coos over her baby. It seemed a long time since she had run away from the *troupe*: she would forget all about them soon, she thought, and their ugly faces. She shivered slightly as she recalled the face of "Le Boss" as it was last bent upon her, frowning and dark, and as ugly as a hundred devils, she was quite sure. Ah, he would take away her violin—Le Boss! he would give it to his own girl, whom she, Marie, had taught till she could play a very little, enough to keep the birds from flying away when they saw her, as they otherwise might; she was to have the violin, the Lady, one's own heart and life, and Marie was to have a fiddle that he had picked up anywhere, found on an ash-heap, most likely! Ah, and now he had lost the Lady and Marie too, and who would play for him this evening, and draw the children out of the houses? he! let some one tell Marie that! It had not been hard, the running away, for no one would ever have thought of Marie's daring to do such a thing. She belonged to Le Boss, as much as the tent or the ponies, or his own ugly girl: so they all thought in the *troupe*, and so Marie herself had thought till that day; that is, she had not thought at all. While she could play all the time, and had often quite enough to eat, and always something, a piece of bread in the hand if no more,—and La Patronne, Le Boss's wife, never too unkind, and sometimes even giving her a bit of ribbon for the Lady's neck when there was to be a special performance,—why, who would have thought of running away? she had been with them so long, those others, and that time in France was so long ago,—hundreds of years ago!

So no one had thought of noticing when she dropped behind to tune her violin and practise by herself; it was a thing she did every day, they all knew, for she could not practise when the children pulled her gown all the time, and wanted to dance. She had chosen the place well, having been on the lookout for it all day, ever since Le Boss told her what he meant to do,—that infamy which the good God would never have allowed, if He had not been perhaps tired with the many infamies of Le Boss, and forgotten to notice this one. She had chosen the place well! A little wood dipped down to the right, with a brook running beyond, and across the brook a sudden sharp rise, crowned with a thick growth of birches. She had played steadily as she passed through the wood and over the stream, and only ceased when she gained the brow of the hill and sprang like a deer down the opposite slope. No one had seen her go, she was sure of that; and now they could never tell which way she had turned, and would be far more likely to run back along the road. How they would shout and scream, and how Le Boss would swear! Ah, no more would he swear at Marie because people did not always give money, being perhaps poor themselves, or unwilling to give to so ugly a face as his girl's, who carried round the dish. No more! And La Patronne would be sorry perhaps a little,—she had the good heart, La Patronne, under all the fat,—and Old Billy, he would be too sorry, she was sure. Poor Old Billy! it was cruel to leave him, when he had such joy of her playing, the good old man, and a hard life taking care of the beasts, and bearing all the blame if any of them died through hunger. But it would have been sadder for Old Billy to see her die, Marie, and she would have died, of course she would! To live without the Lady, a pretty life that would be! far sooner would one go at once to the good God, where the angels played all day, even if one were not allowed to play oneself just at first. Afterward, of course, when they found out how she had played down here, it would be otherwise.

Meanwhile, all these thoughts did not keep Marie from being tired, and hungry too; and she was glad enough to see some brown roofs clustered together at a little distance, as she turned a corner of the road. A village! good! Here would be children, without doubt; and where there were children, Marie was among friends. She stopped for a moment, to push back her hair, which had fallen down in the course of her night, and to tie the blue handkerchief neatly over it, and shake the dust from her bare feet. They were pretty feet, so brown and slender! She had shoes, but they were in the wagon; La Patronne took care of all the Sunday clothes, and there had been no chance to get at anything, even if she could have been hampered by such things as shoes, with the Lady to carry. It did not in the least matter about shoes, when it was summer: when the road was hot, one walked in the cool grass at the side; when there was no grass—eh, one waited till one came to some. They were only for state, these shoes. They were stiff and hard, and the heel-places hurt: it was different for La Patronne, who wore stockings under hers. But here were the houses, and it was time to play. They were pleasant-looking houses, Marie thought, they looked as if persons lived in them who stayed at home and spun, as the women did in Brittany. Ah, that it was far away, Brittany! she had almost forgotten it, and now it all seemed to come back to her, as she gazed about her at the houses, some white, some brown, all with an air of thrift and comfort, as becomes a New England village. That white house there, with the bright green blinds! That pleased her eye. And see! there was a child's toy lying on the step, a child's face peeping out of the window. Decidedly, she had arrived.

Marie took out her violin, and tuned it softly, with little rustling, whispering notes, speaking of perfect accord between owner and instrument; then she looked up at the child and smiled, and began to play "En revenant d'Auvergne." It was a tune that the little people always loved, and when one heard it, the feet began to dance before the head. Sure enough, the door opened in another moment, and the child came slipping out: not with flying steps, as a city child would come, to whom wandering musicians were a thing of every day; but shyly, with sidelong movements, clinging to the wall as it advanced, and only daring by stealth to lift its eyes to the strange woman with the fiddle, a sight never seen before in its little life. But Marie knew all about the things that children think. What was she but a child herself? she had little knowledge of grown persons, and regarded them all as ogres, more or less, except Old Billy, and La Patronne, who really meant to be kind.

"Come, lit' girl!" she said in her clear soft voice. "Come and dance! for you I play, for you I sing too, if you will. Ah, the pretty song, 'En revenant d'Auvergne!'" And she began to sing as she played:

The little girl pressed closer against the wall, her eyes wide open, her finger in her mouth, yet came nearer and nearer, drawn by the smile as well as the music. Presently another came running up, and another; then the boys, who had just brought their cows home and were playing marbles on the sly, behind the brown barn, heard the sound of the fiddle and came running, stuffing their gains into their pockets as they ran. Then Mrs. Piper, who was always foolish about music, her neighbors said, came to her door, and Mrs. Post opposite, who was as deaf as her namesake, came to see what Susan Piper was after, loitering round the door when the men-folks were coming in to their supper: and so with one thing and another, Marie had quite a little crowd around her, and was feeling happy and pleased, and sure that when she stopped playing and carried round her handkerchief knotted at the four corners so as to form a bag, the pennies would drop into it as fast, yes, and maybe a good deal faster, than if Le Boss's ugly daughter was carrying it, with her nose turned up and one eye looking round the corner to see where her hair was gone to. Ah, Le

Boss, what was he doing this evening for his music, with no Marie and no Lady!

And it was just at this triumphant moment that Jacques De Arthenay came round the corner and into the village street.

CHAPTER II.

"D'ARTHENAY, TENEZ FOI!"

There had been De Arthenays in the village ever since it became a village: never many of them, one or two at most in a generation; not a prolific stock, but a hardy and persistent one. No one knew when the name had dropped its soft French sound, and taken the harsh Anglo-Saxon accent. It had been so with all the old French names, the L'Homme-Dieus and Des Isles and Beaulieus; the air, or the granite, or one knows not what, caused an ossification of the consonants, a drying up of the vowels, till these names, once soft and melodious, became more angular, more rasping in utterance, than ever Smith or Jones could be.

They were Huguenots, the d'Arthenays. A friend from childhood of St. Castin, Jacques d'Arthenay had followed his old companion to America at the time when the revocation of the Edict of Nantes rendered France no safe dwelling-place for those who had no hinges to their knees. A stern, silent man, this d'Arthenay, like most of his race: holding in scorn the things of earthly life, brooding over grievances, given to dwelling much on heaven and hell, as became his time and class. Leaving castle and lands and all earthly ties behind them, he and his wife came out of Sodom, as they expressed it, and turned not their faces, looking steadfastly forward to the wilderness where they were to worship God in His own temple, the virgin forest. It had been a terrible shock to find the Baron de St. Castin fallen away from religion and civilisation, living in savage pomp with his savage wives, the daughters of the great chief Modocawando. There could be no such companionship as this for the Sieur d'Arthenay and his noble wife; the friendship of half a lifetime was sternly repudiated, and d'Arthenay cast in his lot with the little band of Huguenot settlers who were striving to win their livelihood from the rugged soil of eastern Maine.

It was bitter bread that they ate, those French settlers. We read the story again and again, each time with a fresh pang of pity and regret; but it is not of them that this tale is told. Jacques d'Arthenay died in his wilderness, and his wife followed him quickly, leaving a son to carry on the name. The gravestone of these first d'Arthenays was still to be seen in the old burying-ground: they had been the first to be buried there. The old stone was sunk half-way in the earth, and was gray with moss and lichens; but the inscription was still legible, if one looked close, and had patience to decipher the crabbed text.

7

"Jacques St. George, Sieur d'Arthenay et de Vivonne. Mort en foi et en esperance, 28me Decembre, 1694."

Then a pair of mailed hands, clasped as in sign of friendship or loyalty, and beneath them again, the words,

"D'Arthenay, tenez foi!"

The story was that the son of this first Sieur d'Arthenay had been exposed to some dire temptation, whether of love or of ambition was not clearly known, and had been in danger of turning from the faith of his people and embracing that of Rome. He came one day to meditate beside his father's grave, hoping perhaps to draw some strength, some inspiration, from the memories of that stern and righteous Huguenot; and as he sat beside the stone, lo! a mailed hand appeared, holding a sword, and graved with the point of the sword on the stone, the old motto of his father's house,—

"D'Arthenay, tenez foi!"

And he had been strengthened, and lived and died in the faith of his father. Many people in the village scouted this story, and called it child's foolishness, but there were some who liked to believe it, and who pointed out that these words were not carved deeply and regularly, like the rest of the inscription, but roughly scratched, as if with a sharp point. And that although merely so scratched, they had never been effaced, but were even more easily read than the carven script.

Among those who held it for foolishness was the present Jacques De Arthenay. He was perhaps the fifth in descent from the old Huguenot, but he might have been his own son or brother. The Huguenot doctrines had only grown a little colder, a little harder, turned into New England Orthodoxy as it was understood fifty years ago. He thought little of his French descent or his noble blood. He pronounced his name Jakes, as all his neighbors did; he lived on his farm, as they lived on theirs. If it was a better farm, the land in better condition, the buildings and fences trimmer and better cared for, that was in the man, not in his circumstances. He was easily leader among the few men whose scattered dwellings made up the village of Sea Meadows (commonly pronounced Semedders.) His house did not lie on the little "street," as that part of the road was called where some half-dozen houses were clustered together, with their farms spreading out behind them, and the post-office for the kingpin; yet no important step would be taken by the villagers without the advice and approval of Jacques De Arthenay. Briefly, he was a born leader; a masterful man, with a habit of thinking before he spoke; and when he said a thing must be done, people were apt to do it. He was now thirty years old, without kith or kin that any one knew of; living by himself in a good house, and keeping it clean and decent, almost as a woman might; not likely ever to change his condition, it was supposed.

This was the man who happened to come into the street on some errand, that soft summer evening, at the very moment when Marie was feeling lifted up by the light of joy in the children's faces, and was telling herself how good it was that she had come this way. Hearing the sound of the fiddle, De Arthenay stopped for a moment, and his face grew dark as night. He was a religious man, as sternly so as his Huguenot ancestor, but wearing his religion with a difference. He knew all music, except psalm-tunes, to be directly from the devil. Even as to the psalm-tunes themselves, it seemed to him a dreadful thing that worship could not be conducted without this compromise with evil, this snare to catch the ear; and he harboured in the depth of his soul thoughts about the probable frivolity of David, which he hardly voiced even to himself. The fiddle, in particular, he held to be positively devilish, both in its origin and influence; those who played this unholy instrument were bound to no good place, and were sure to gain their port, in his opinion. Being thus minded, it was with a shock of horror that he heard the sound of a fiddle in the street of his own village, not fifty yards from the meeting-house itself. After a moment's pause, he came wrathfully down the street; his height raised him a head and shoulders above the people who were ringed around the little musician, and he looked over their heads, with his arm raised to command, and his lips opened to forbid the shameful thing. Then—he saw Marie's face; and straightway his arm dropped to his side, and he stood without speaking. The children looked up at him, and moved away, for they were always afraid of him, and at this moment his face was dreadful to see.

Yet it was nothing dreadful that he looked upon. Marie was standing with her head bent down over her violin, in a pretty way she had. A light, slight figure, not short, yet with a look that spoke all of youth and morning grace. She wore a little blue gown, patched and faded, and dusty enough after her day's walk; her feet were dusty too, but slender and delicately shaped. Her face was like nothing that had been seen in those parts before, and the beauty of it seemed to strike cold to the man's heart, as he stood and gazed with unwilling eyes, hating the feeling that constrained him, yet unable for the moment to restrain it or to turn his eyes away. She had that clear, bright whiteness of skin that is seen only in Frenchwomen, and only here and there among these; whiteness as of fire behind alabaster. Her hair was black and soft, and the lashes lay like jet on her cheek, as she stood looking down, smiling a little, feeling so happy, so pleased that she was pleasing others. And now, when she raised her eyes, they were seen to be dark and soft, too; but with what fire in their depths, what sunny light of joy,—the joy of a child among children! De Arthenay started, and his hands clenched themselves unconsciously. Marie started, too, as she met the stern gaze fixed upon her, and the joyous light faded from her eyes. Rudely it broke in upon her pleasant thoughts,—this vision of a set, bearded face, with cold blue eyes that yet had a flame in them, like a spark struck from steel. The little song died on her lips, and unconsciously she lowered her bow, and stood silent, returning helplessly the look bent so sternly upon her.

When Jacques de Arthenay found himself able to speak at last, he started at the sound of his own voice.

"Who are you?" he asked. "How did you come here, young woman?"

Marie held out her fiddle with a pretty, appealing gesture. "I come—from away!" she said, in her broken English, that sounded soft and strange to his ears. "I do no harm. I play, to make happy the children, to get bread for me."

"Who came with you?" De Arthenay continued. "Who are your folks?"

Marie shook her head, and a light crept into her eyes as she thought of Le Boss. "I have nobodies'" she said. "I am with myself, *sauf le violon*; I mean, wiz my fiddle. Monsieur likes not music, no?"

She looked wistfully at him, and something seemed to rise up in the man's throat and choke him. He made a violent motion, as if to free himself from something. What had happened to him,—was he suddenly possessed, or was he losing his wits? He tried to force his voice back into its usual tone, tried even to speak gently, though his heart was beating so wildly at the way she looked, at the sweet notes of her voice, like a flute in its lower notes, that he could hardly hear his own words. "No, no music!" he said. "There must be no music here, among Christian folks. Put away that thing, young woman. It is an evil thing, bringing sin, and death, which is the wages of sin, with it. How came you here, if you have no one belonging to you?"

10

Falteringly, her sweet eyes dropped on the ground, with only now and then a timid, appealing glance at this terrible person, this awful judge who had suddenly dropped from the skies, Marie told her little story, or as much of it as she thought needful. She had been with bad people, playing for them, a long time, she did not know how long. And then they would take away her violin, and she would not stay, and she ran away from them, and had walked all day, and—and that was all. A little sob shook her voice at the last words; she had not realised before how utterly alone she was. The delight of freedom, of getting away from her tyrants, had been enough at first, and she had been as it were on wings all day, like a bird let loose from its cage; now the little bird was weary, and the wings drooped, and there was no nest, not even a friendly cage where one would find food and drink,

A sudden passion of pity—he supposed it was pity—shook the strong man. He felt a wild impulse to catch the little shrinking creature in his arms and bear her away to his own home, to warm and cheer and comfort her. Was there ever before anything in the world so sweet, so helpless, so forlorn? He looked around. The children were all gone; he stood alone in the street with the foreign woman, and night was falling. It was at this moment that Abby Rock, who had been watching from her window for the past few minutes, opened her door and came out, stepping quietly toward them, as if they were just the people she had expected to see. De Arthenay hailed her as an angel from Heaven; and yet Abby did not look like an angel.

"Abby!" he cried. "Come here a minute, will you?"

"Good evening, Jacques!" said Abby, in her quiet voice. "Good evening to you!" she added, speaking kindly to the little stranger. "I was coming to see if you wouldn't like to step into my house and rest you a spell. Why, my heart!" she cried, as Marie raised her head at the sound of the friendly voice, "you're nothing but a child. Come right along with me, my dear. Alone, are ye, and night coming on!"

"That's right, Abby!" cried De Arthenay, with feverish eagerness. "Yes, yes, take her home with you and make her comfortable. She is a stranger, and has no friends, so she says. I—I'll see you in the morning about her. Take her! take her in where she will be comfortable, and I'll—"

"I'll pay you well for it," was what he was going to say, but Abby's quiet look stopped the words on his lips. Why should he pay her for taking care of a

11

stranger, of whom he knew no more than she did; whom he had never seen till this moment?—why, indeed! and she was as well able to pay for the young woman's keep as he was to say the least. All this De Arthenay saw, or fancied he saw, in Abby Rock's glance. He turned away, muttering something about seeing them in the morning; then, with an abrupt bow, which yet was not without grace, he strode swiftly down the street and took his way home.

CHAPTER III.

ABBY ROCK.

If Abby Rock's kitchen was not heaven, it seemed very near it to Marie that evening. She found herself suddenly in an atmosphere of peace and comfort of which her life had heretofore known nothing. The evening had fallen chill outside, but here all was warm and light and cheerful, and the warmth and cheer seemed to be embodied in the person of the woman who moved quickly to and fro, stirring the fire, putting the kettle on the hob (for those were the days of the open fire, of crane and kettle, and picturesque, if not convenient, housekeeping), drawing a chair up near the cheerful blaze. Marie felt herself enfolded with comfort. A shawl was thrown over her shoulders; she was lifted like a child, and placed in the chair by the fireside; and now, as she sat in a dream, fearing every moment to wake and find herself back in the old life again, a cup of tea, hot and fragrant, was set before her, and the handkerchief tenderly loosened from her neck, while a kind voice bade her drink, for it would do her good.

"You look beat out, and that's the fact," said Abby Rock. "To-morrow you shall tell me all about it, but you no need to say a single word to-night, only just set still and rest ye. I'm a lone woman here. I buried my mother last June, and I'm right glad to have company once in a while. Abby Rock, my name is; and perhaps if you'd tell me yours, we should feel more comfortable like, when we come to sit down to supper. What do you say?"

Her glance was so kind, her voice so cordial and hearty, that Marie could have knelt down to thank her. "I am Marie," she said, smiling back into the kind eyes. "Only Marie, nossing else."

"Maree!" repeated Abby Rock. "Well, it's a pretty name, sure enough; has a sound of 'Mary' in it, too, and that was my mother's name. But what was your father's name, or your mother's, if so be your father ain't living now?"

Marie shook her head. "I never know!" she said. "All the days I lived with Mere Jeanne in the village, far away, oh, far, over the sea."

"Over the sea?" said Abby. "You mean the bay, don't you,—some of those French settlements down along the shore?"

But Marie meant the sea, it appeared; for her village was in France, in Eretagne, and there she had lived till the day when Mere Jeanne died, and she was left alone, with no-one belonging to her. Mere Jeanne was not her mother, no! nor yet her grandmother,—only her mother's aunt, but good, Abby must understand, good as an angel, good as Abby herself. And when she was dead, there was only her son, Jeannot, and he had married a devil,—but yes!—as Abby exclaimed, and held up her hands in reproof,—truly a devil of the worst kind; and one day, when Jeannot was away, this wife had sold her, Marie, to another devil, Le Boss, who made the tours in the country for to sing and to play. And he had brought her away to this country, over very dreadful seas, where one went down into the grave at every instant, and then up again to the clouds, but leaving one's stomach behind one—ah, but terrible! Others were with them, oh, yes!—This in response to Abby's question, for in spite of her good resolutions, curiosity was taking possession of her, and it was evidently a relief to Marie to pour out her little tale in a sympathetic ear,—many others. La Patronne, the wife of Le Boss, who was like a barrel, but not bad, when she could see through the fat, not bad in every way; and there was Old Billy, who took care of the horses and dogs, and he was her friend, and she loved him, and he had always the good word for her even when he was very drunk, too drunk to speak to any one else. And then there was the daughter of Le Boss, who would in all probability never die, for she was so ugly that she would not be admitted into the other world, where, Mere Jeanne said, even Monsieur the Great Devil himself was good-looking, save for his expression. Also there were the boys who tumbled and rode on the ponies, and—and—and ozer people. And with this Mane's head dropped forward, and she was asleep.

It seemed a pity to wake her when supper was ready, but Abby knew just how good her rolls were, and knew that the child must be famished; and sure enough, after a little nap, Marie was ready to wake and sit up at the little round table, and be fed like a baby with everything good that Abby could think of. The fare had not been dainty in the travelling troupe of Le Boss. The fine white bread, the golden butter, the bit of broiled fish, smoking hot, seemed viands of paradise to the hungry girl. She laughed for pleasure, and her eyes shone like stars. It was like the chateau, she said, where everything was gold and silver,—the chateau where Madame la Comtesse lived. As for Abby herself, Marie gravely informed her that she was an angel. Abby laughed, not ill pleased. "I don't look special like angels," she said; "that is, if the pictures I've seen are correct. Not much wings and curls and white robes about me, Maree. And who ever heard of an angel in a check apurn, I want to know?"

14

But Marie was not to be turned aside. It was well known, she said, that angels could not come to earth undisguised in these days. It had something to do with the Jews, she did not know exactly what. Mere Jeanne had told her, but she forgot just how it was. But as to their not coming at all, that would be out of the question, for how would the good God know what was going on down here, or know who was behaving well and meriting a crown of glory, and who should go down into the pit? Did not Abby see that?

Abby privately thought that here was strange heathen talk to be going on in her kitchen; but she said nothing, only gave her guest more jam, and said she was eating nothing,—the proper formula for a good hostess, no matter how much the guest may have devoured.

It was true, as has been said before, that Abby Rock was not fair to outward view. Nature had been in a crabbed mood when she fashioned this gaunt, angular form, these gnarled, unlovely features. An uncharitable neighbour, in describing Abby, once said that she looked as if she had swallowed an old cedar fence-rail and shrunk to it; and the description was apt enough so far as the body went. Her skin, eyes, and hair were of different shades (yet not so very different) of greyish brown; her nose was long and knotty, her mouth and chin apparently taken at random from a box of misfits. Yes, the cedar fence-rail came as near to it as anything could. Yet somehow, no one who had seen the light of kindness in those faded eyes, and heard the sweet, cordial tones of that quiet voice, thought much about their owner's looks. People said it was a pity Abby wasn't better favoured, and then they thought no more about it, but were simply thankful that she existed.

She had led the life that many an ugly saint leads, here in New England, and the world over. Nurse and drudge for the pretty younger sister, the pride and joy of her heart, till she married and went away to live in a distant State; then drudge and nurse for the invalid mother, broken down by unremitting toil. No toil would ever break Abby down, for she was a strong woman; she had never worked too hard that she was aware of; but—she had always worked, and never done anything else. No lover had ever looked into her eyes or taken her hand tenderly. Not likely! she would say to herself with a scornful sniff, eyeing her homely face in the glass. Men weren't such fools as they looked.

One or two had wanted to marry her house, as she expressed it, and had asked for herself into the bargain, not seeing how they could manage it otherwise. They were not to blame for wanting the house, she thought with some complacency, as she glanced round her sitting-room. Everything in the room shone and twinkled. The rugs were beautifully made, and the floor under them in the usual dining-table condition ascribed ever since books were written to the model housewife. The corner cupboards held treasures of blue and white that it makes one ache to think of to-day, and some pieces of India china besides, brought over seas by some sea-going Rock of a former generation: and there were silver spoons in the iron box under Abby's bed, and the dragon tea-pot on the high narrow mantel-piece was always full, but not with tea-leaves. Yes, and there was no better cow in the village than Abby's, save those two fancy heifers that Jacques de Arthenay had lately bought. Altogether, she did not wonder that some of the weaker brethren, who found their own farms "hard sledding," should think enough of her pleasant home to be willing to take her along with it, since they could do no better; but they did not get it. Abby found life very pleasant, now that grief was softened down into tender recollection. To be alone, and able to do things just when she wanted to do them, and in her own way; to consider what she herself liked to eat, and to wear, and to do; to feel that she could come and go, rise up and lie down, at her own will,—was strange but pleasant to her. How long the pleasure would have lasted is another question, for the woman's nature was to love and to serve; but just now there was no doubt that she was enjoying her freedom.

And now she had taken in this little stranger, just because she felt like it; it was a new luxury, a new amusement, that was all. Such a pretty little creature, so soft and young, and with that brightness in her face! Sister Lizzie was light-complected, and this child didn't favour her, not the least mite; yet it was some like the same feeling, as if it were a kitten or a pretty bird to take care of, and feed and pet. So thought Abby, as she tucked up Marie in Sister Lizzie's little white bed, in the pink ribbon chamber, as she had named it in sport, after she had let Lizzie furnish it to her taste, that last year before she was married. The child looked about her as if it were a palace, instead of a lean-to chamber with a sloping roof. She had never seen anything like this in her life, since those days when she went to the chateau. She touched the white walls softly, and passed her hand over the pink mats on the bureau with wondering awe. And then she curled up in the white bed when Abby bade her, as like a kitten as anything could be. "Oh, you are good, good!" cried the child, whom the warmth and comfort and kindness seemed to have lifted into another world from the cold, sordid one in which she had lived so long. She caught the kind hard knotted hand, and kissed it; but Abby snatched it away, and blushed to her eyebrows, feeling that something improper had occurred. "There! there!" she said, half confused, half reproving. "You don't want to do such things as that!

16

I've done no more than was right, and you alone and friendless, and night coming on. Go to sleep now, like a good girl, and we'll see in the morning." So Marie went to sleep in Sister Lizzie's bed, with her fiddle lying across her feet, since she could not sleep a wink otherwise, she said; and when Abby went downstairs the room seemed cold, and she thought how she missed Lizzie, and wondered if it wouldn't be pleasant to keep this pretty creature for a spell, and do for her a little, and make her up some portion of clothing. There was a real good dress of Lizzie's, hanging this minute in the press upstairs: she had a good mind to take it out at once and see what could be done to it; perhaps— and Abby did not go to bed very early herself that night.

CHAPTER IV.

POSSESSION.

Jacques De Arthenay went home that night like a man possessed. He was furious with himself, with the strange woman who had thus set his sober thoughts in a whirl, with the very children in the street who had laughed and danced and encouraged her in her sinful music, to her own peril and theirs. He thought it was only anger that so held his mind; yet once in his house, seated on the little stool before his fire, he found himself still in the street, still looking down into that lovely childish face that lifted itself so innocently to his, still smitten to the heart by the beauty of it, and by the fear that he saw in it of his own stern aspect. He had never looked upon any woman before. He had been proud of it,—proud of his strength and cleverness, that needed no meddlesome female creature coming in between him and his business, between him and his religion. He had not let his hair and beard grow, knowing nothing of such practices, but in heart he had been a Nazarite from his youth up,—serving God in his harsh, unloving way; loving God, as he thought; certainly loving nothing else, if it were not the dumb creatures, to whom he was always kind and just. And now—what had happened to him? He asked himself the question sternly, sitting there before the cheerful blaze, yet neither seeing nor feeling it. The answer seemed to cry itself in his ears, to write itself before his eyes in letters of fire. The thing had happened that happens in the story books, that really comes to pass once in a hundred years, they say. He had seen the one woman in the world that he wanted for his own, to have and to hold, to love and to cherish. She was a stranger, a vagabond, trading in iniquity, and gaining her bread by the corruption of souls of men and children; and he loved her, he longed for her, and the world meant nothing to him henceforth unless he could have her. He put the thought away from him like a snake, but it came back and curled round his heart, and made him cold and then hot and then cold again. Was he not a professing Christian, bound by the strictest ties? Yes! How she looked, standing there with the children about her, the little slender figure swaying to and fro to the music, the pretty head bent down so lovingly, the dark eyes looking here and there, bright and shy, like those of a wild creature so gentle in its nature that it knew no fear. But he had taught her fear! yes, he saw it grow under his eyes, just as the love grew in his own heart at the same moment.

Love! what sort of word was that for him to be using, even in his mind? To-morrow she would be gone, this wandering fiddler, and all this would be forgotten in a day, for he had the new cattle to see to, and a hundred things of importance.

But was anything else of importance save just this one girl? and if he should let her go on her way, out into the world again, to certain perdition, would not the guilt be partly his? He, who saw and knew the perils and pitfalls, might he not snatch this child from the fire and save her soul alive?—No! he would begone, as soon as morning came, and take this sinful body of his away from temptation.

How soon would Abby get through her morning work, so that he might with some fair pretext go to the house to see how the stranger had slept, and how she had fared? It would be cowardly to drop the burden on Abby's shoulders, she only a woman like the rest of them, even if she had somewhat more sense.

So Jacques De Arthenay sat by his fire till it was cold and dead, a miserable and a wrathful man; and he too slept little that night.

But Marie slept long and peacefully in Sister Lizzie's bed, and looked so pretty in her sleep that Abby came three times to wake her, and three times went away again, unable to spoil so perfect a picture. At last, however, the dark eyes opened of their own accord, and Marie began to chirp and twitter, like a bird at daybreak in its nest; only instead of daybreak, it was eight o'clock in the morning, a most shocking hour for anybody to be getting up. But Abby had been in the habit of spoiling her sister, who had a theory that she was never able to do anything early in the morning, and so it was much more considerate for her to stay in bed and keep out of Abby's way. This is a comfortable theory.

"I suppose you've been an early riser, though?" said Abby, as she poured the coffee, looking meanwhile approvingly at the figure of her guest, neatly attired in a pink and white print gown, which fitted her in a truly astonishing manner, proving, Abby thought in her simple way, that it had really been a "leading,"— her bringing the stranger home last night.

"Oh, but yes," Marie answered. "I help always Old Billy wiz the dogs first, they must be exercise, and do their tricks, and then they are feed. So hungry they are, the dogs! It make very hard not first to feed them, *hein*?"

"Is—William—feeble?" Abby inquired, with some hesitation.

"Feeble, no!" said Marie, with a little laugh. "But old, you know, and when he is too much drunk it take away his mind; so then I help him, that Le Boss does not find out that and beat him. For he is good, you see, Old Billy, and we make comrades togezzer always."

"Dear me!" said Abby, doubtfully. "It don't seem as if you ought to be going with—with that kind of person, Maree. We don't associate with drinking men, here in these parts. I don't know how it is where you come from."

Oh, there, Marie said, it was different. There the drink did not make men crazy. This was a country where the devil had so much power, you see, that it made it hard for poor folks like Old Billy, who would do well enough in her country, and at the worst take a little too much at a feast or a wedding. But in those cases, the saints took very good care that nothing should happen to them. She did not know what the saints did in this country, or indeed, if there were any.

"Oh, Maree!" cried Abby, scandalised. "I guess I wouldn't talk like that, if I was you. You—you, ain't a papist, are you,—a Catholic?"

Oh, no! Mere Jeanne was of the Reformed religion, and had brought Marie up so. It was a misfortune, Madame the Countess always said; but Marie preferred to be as Mere Jeanne had been. The Catholic girls in the village said that Mere Jeanne had gone straight to the pit, but that proved that they were ignorant entirely of the things of religion. Why, Le Boss was a Catholic, he; and everybody knew that he had the evil eye, and that it was not safe to come near him without making the horns.

"For the land's sake!" cried Abby Rock, dropping her dish-cloth into the sink, "what are you talking about, child?"

"But, the horns!" Marie answered innocently. "When a person has the evil eye, you not make at him the horns, so way?" and she held out the index and little finger of her right hand, bending the other fingers down. "So!" she said; "when they so are held, the evil eye has no power. What you do here to stop him?"

"We don't believe in any such a thing!" Abby replied, with, some severity. "Why, Maree, them's all the same as heathen notions, like witchcraft and such. We don't hold by none of those things in this country at all, and I guess you'd better not talk about 'em."

Marie's eyes opened wide. "But," she said, "*c'est une chose,*—it is a thing that all know. As for Le Boss, you know—listen!" she came nearer to Abby, and lowered her voice. "One night Old Billy forgot to do, I know not what, but somesing. So when Le Boss found it out, he look at him, so,"—drawing her brows down and frowning horribly, with the effect of looking like an enraged kitten,—"and say noasing at all. You see?"

"Well," replied Abby. "I suppose mebbe he thought it was an accident, and might have happened to any one."

"Not—at—all!" cried Marie, with dramatic emphasis, throwing out her hand with a solemn gesture. "What happen that same night? Old Billy fall down the bank and break his leg!" She paused, and nodded like a little mandarin, to point the moral of her tale.

"Maree!" remonstrated Abby Rock, "don't tell me you believe such foolishness as that! He'd have fallen down all the same if nobody had looked anigh him. Why, good land! I never heard of such notions."

"So it is!" Marie insisted. "Le Boss look at him, and he break his leg. I see the break! Anozer day," she continued, "Coco, he is a boy that makes tumble, and he was hungry, and he took a don't from the table to eat it—"

"Took a what?" asked Abby.

"A don't, what you call. Round, wiz a hole to put your finger!" explained Marie. "Only in America they make zem. Not of such things in Bretagne, never. Coco took the don't, and Le Boss catch him, and look at him again, so! Well, yes! in two hour he is sick, that boy, and after zat for a week. A-a-a-h! yes, Le Boss! only at me he not dare to look, for I have the charm, and he know that, and he is afraid. Aha, yes, he is afraid of Marie too, when he wish to make devil work.

"And here," she cried, turning suddenly upon Abby, "you say you have no such thing, Abiroc,"—this was the name she had given her hostess,—"and here, too, is the evil eye, first what I see in this place, except the dear little children. A man yesterday came while I played, and looked—but, frightful! Ah!" she started from her seat by the window, and retreated hastily to the corner. "He comes, the same man! Put me away, Abiroc! put me away! He is bad, he is wicked! I die if he look at me!" and she ran hastily out of the room, just as Jacques De Arthenay entered it.

CHAPTER V.

COURTSHIP.

Marie could hardly be persuaded to come back into the sitting-room; and when she did at length come, it was only to sit silent in the corner, with one hand held behind her, and her eyes fixed steadfastly on the floor. In vain Abby Rock tried to draw her into the conversation, telling her how she, Abby, and Mr. De Arthenay had been talking about her, and how they thought she'd better stay right on where she was for a spell, till she was all rested up, and knew what she wanted to do. Mr. De Arthenay would be a friend to her, and no one could be a better one, as she'd find. But Marie only said that Monsieur was very kind, and never raised her eyes to his. De Arthenay, on his part, was no more at ease. He could not take his eyes from the slender figure, so shrinking and modest, or the lovely downcast face. He had no words to tell her all that was in his heart, nor would he have told it if he could. It was still a thing of horror to him,—a thing that would surely be cast out as soon as he came to himself; and how better could he bring himself to his senses than by facing this dream, this possession of the night, and crushing it down, putting it out of existence? So he sat still, and gazed at the dream, and felt its reality in every fibre of his being; and poor good Abby sat and talked for all three, and wondered what to goodness was coming of all this.

She wondered more and more as the days went on. It became evident to her that De Arthenay, her stern, silent neighbour, who had never so much as looked at a woman before, was "possessed" about her little guest. Marie, on the other hand, continued to regard him with terror, and never failed to make the horns secretly when he appeared; yet day after day he came, and sat silent in the sitting-room, and gazed at Marie, and wrestled with the devil within him. He never doubted that it was the devil. There was no awkwardness to him in sitting thus silent; it was the habit of his life: he spoke when he had occasion to say anything; for the rest, he considered over-much speech as one of the curses of our fallen state. But Abby "felt as if she should fly," as she expressed it to herself, while he sat there. A pall of silence seemed to descend upon the room, generally so cheerful: the French girl cowered under it, and seemed to shrink visibly, like a dumb creature in fright. And when he was gone, she would spring up and run like a deer to her own little room, and seize her violin, and play passionately, the instrument crying under her hands, like a living creature, protesting against grief, against silence and darkness, and the fear of something unknown, which seemed to be growing out of the silence.

Sometimes Abby thought the best thing to do would be to open the door of the cage, and let the little stray bird flutter out, as she had fluttered in those few days ago, by chance—was it by chance?

But the bird was so willing to stay; was so happy, except when that silent shadow fell upon the cheerful house; so sweet, so grateful for little kindnesses (and who would not be kind to her, Abby thought!); such a singing, light, pretty creature to look at and listen to! and the house had been so quiet since mother died; and after all, it was pleasant to have some one to do for and "putter round." The neighbours said, There! now Abby Rock was safe to live, for she had got another baby to take care of; she'd ha' withered up and blown away if she had gone on living alone, with no one to make of.

And what talks they had, Abby and Marie! The latter told all about her early childhood with the good old woman whom she called Mere Jeanne, and explained how she came to have the Lady, and to play as she did. The Countess, it appeared, lived up at the castle; a great lady, oh, but very great, and beautiful as the angels. She was alone there, for the Count was away on a foreign mission, and she had no child, the Countess. So one day she saw Marie, when the latter was bringing flowers to the gardener's wife, who was good to her; and the Countess called the child to her, and took her on her knee, and talked with her. Ah, she was good, the Countess, and lovely! After that Marie was brought to the castle every day, and the Countess played to her of the violin, and Marie knew all at once that this was the best thing in the world, and the dearest, and the one to die for, you understand. (But Abby did not understand in the least.) So when Madame the Countess saw how it was, she taught Marie, and got her the Lady, the violin which was Marie's life and soul; and she let come down from Paris a great teacher, and they all played together, the Countess his friend, for many years his pupil, and the great violinist, and Marie, the little peasant girl in her blue gown and cap. He said she was a born musician, Marie: of course, he was able to see things, being of the same nature; but Mere Jeanne was unhappy, and said no good would come of it. Yes, well, what is to be, you know, that will be, and nossing else. The great teacher died, and there was an end of him. And after a while Monsieur the Count came home, and carried away the Countess to live in Paris, and so— and—so—that was all!

"But not all!" cried the child, springing from her seat, and raising her head, which had drooped for a moment. "Not all! for I have the music, see, Abiroc! All days of my life I can make music, make happy, make joy of myself and

23

ozerbodies. When I take her; Madame, so, in my hand, I can do what I will, no? People have glad thinks, sorry thinks; what Marie tells them to have, that have they. *Ah! la tonne aventure, oh gai!*" and she would throw her head back and begin to play, and play till the chairs almost danced on their four legs.

De Arthenay never heard the fiddle. Abby managed it somehow, she hardly knew how or why. He had never spoken about the Evil Thing, as he would have called it, since that first day; perhaps he thought that Abby had taken it away, as a pious church member should, and destroyed it from the face of the earth. At all events there was no mention of it, and the only sound he heard when he approached the house was the whir of Abby's wheel (for women still spun then, in that part of the country), or the one voice he cared to hear in the world, uplifted in some light godless song.

So things went on for a while; and then came a change. One day Marie came into the sitting-room, hearing Abby call her. It was the hour of De Arthenay's daily visit, and he sat silent in the corner, as usual; but Abby had an open letter in her hand, and was crying softly, with her apron hiding her good homely face. "Maree," said the good woman, "I've got bad news. My sister Lizzie that I've told you so much about, she's dreadful sick, and I've got to go right out and take care of her. Thank you, dear!" (as she felt Marie's arms round her on the instant, and the soft voice murmured little French sympathies in her ear), "you're real good, I'm sure, and I know you feel for me. I've got to go right off to-morrow or next day, soon as I can get things to rights and see to the stock and things. But what is troubling me is you, Maree. I don't see what is to become of you, poor child, unless— Well, now, you come here and sit down by me, and listen to what Mr. De Arthenay has to say to you. You know he's ben your friend, Maree, ever sence you come; so you listen to him, like a good girl."

Abby was in great trouble: indeed, she was the most agitated of the three, for it was with outward calm, at least, that De Arthenay spoke; and Marie listened quietly, too, plaiting her apron, between her fingers, and forgetting for the moment to make the horns with her left hand. Briefly, he asked her to be his wife; to come home with him, and keep his house, and share good and evil with him. He would take care of her, he said, and—and—he trusted the Lord would bless the union. If his voice shook now and then, if he kept his eyes lowered, that neither woman should see the light and the struggle in them, that was his own affair; he spoke quietly to the end, and then drew a long breath, feeling that he had come through better than he had expected.

Abby looked for an outburst of some kind from Marie, whether of tears or of sudden childish fear or anger; but neither came. Marie thanked Monsieur, and said he was very kind, very kind indeed. She would like to think about it a little, if they pleased; she would do all she could to please them, but she was very young, and she would like to take time, if Monsieur thought it not wrong: and so rising from her seat, she made a little courtesy, with her eyes still on the ground, and slipped away out of the room, and was gone.

The others sat looking at each other, neither ready to speak first. Finally Abby reflected that Jacques would not speak, at all unless she began, so she said, with a sigh between the words; "I guess it'll be all right, Jacques. It's only proper that she should have time to think it over, and she such a child. Not but what it's a great chance for her," she added hastily. "My! to get a good home, and a good provider, as I make no doubt you would be, after the life she's led, traipsin' here and there, and livin' with darkened heathens, or as bad. But— but—you'll be kind to her, won't you, Jacques? She—she's not a woman yet, in her feelin's, as you might say. She ain't nothin' but a baby to our girls about here, that's brought up to see with their eyes and talk with their mouths. You'll have patience with her, if her ways are a good deal different from what you were used to; along back in your mother's time?"

But here good Abby paused, for she saw that De Arthenay heard not a word of her well-meant discourse. He sat brooding in the corner, as was his wont, but with a light in his eyes and a color in his cheek that Abby had never seen before.

"Jacques De Arthenay, you are fairly possessed!" she said, in rather an awestruck voice, as he rose abruptly to bid her good-day. "I don't believe you can think of anything except that child."

"So more I can!" said the man, looking at her with bright, hard eyes. "Nothing else! She is my life!" and with that he turned hastily to the door and was gone.

"His life!" repeated Abby, gazing after him as he strode away down the street. "Much like his life she is, the pretty creetur! And she saying that fiddle was her life, only yesterday! How are all these lives going to work together? that's what I want to know!" And she shook her head, and went back to her spinning. There was no doubt in Abby's mind about Marie's answer, when she grew a little used to the new idea. Her silent suitor was many years older than she, it was true, but as she said to him, what a chance for the friendless wanderer! And if he loved her now, how much more he would love her when he came to know her well, and see all her pretty ways about the house, like a kitten or a bird. And she would respect and admire him, that was certain, Abby thought. He was a pictur' of a man, when he got his store clothes on, and nobody had ever had a word to say against him. He was no talker, but some thought that was no drawback in the married state. Abby remembered how Sister Lizzie's young husband had tormented her with foolish questions during the week he bad spent with them at the time of the marriage: a spruce young clerk from a city store, not knowing one end of a hoe from the other, and asking questions all the time, and not remembering anything you told him long enough for it to get inside his head; though there was room enough inside for consid'able many ideas, Abby thought. Yes, certainly, if so be one had to be portioned with a husband, the one that said least would be the least vexation in the end. So she was content, on the whole, and glad that Marie took it all so quietly and sensibly, and made no doubt the girl was turning it over in her mind, and making ready a real pretty answer for Jacques when he called the next day.

Yes, Marie was turning it over in her mind, but not just in the way her good hostess supposed. Only one thought came to her, but that thought filled her whole mind; she must get away,—away at once from this place, from the stern man with the evil eye, who wanted to take her and kill her slowly, that he might have the pleasure of seeing her die. Ah, she knew, Marie! had she not seen wicked people before? But she would not tell Abiroc, for it would only grieve her, and she would talk, talk, and Marie wanted no talking. She only wanted to get away, out into the open fields once more, where nobody would look at her or want to marry her, and where roads might be found leading away to golden cities, full of children who liked to hear play the violin, and who danced when one played it well.

Early next morning, while Abby was out milking the cows, Marie stole away. She put on her little blue gown again; ah! how old and faded it looked beside the fresh, pretty-prints that Abby would always have her wear! But it was her own, and when she had it on, and the old handkerchief tied under her chin once more, and Madame in her box, ready to go with her the world over, why, then she felt that she was Marie once more; that this had all been a mistake, this sojourn among the strange, kind people who spoke so loud and through such long noses; that now her life was to begin, as she had really meant it to begin when she ran away from Le Boss and his hateful tyranny.

Out she slipped, in the sweet, fresh morning. No-one saw her go, for the village was a busy place at all times, and at this early hour every man and woman was busy in barn or kitchen. At one house a child knocked at the window, a child for whom she had played and sung many times. He stood there in his little red nightgown, and nodded and laughed; and Marie nodded back, smiling, and wondered if he would ever run away, and ever know how good, how good it was, to be alone, with no one else in the world to say, "Do this!" or "Do that!" Just as she came out, the sun rose over the hill, and looking at the fiery ball Marie perceived that it danced in the sky. Yes, assuredly, so it was! There was the same wavering motion that she had seen on every fair Easter Day that she could remember. She thought how Mere Jeanne had first called her attention, to it, when she was little, little, just able to toddle, and had told her that the sun danced so on Easter Morning, for joy that the Good Lord had risen from the dead; and so it was a lesson for us all, and we must dance on Easter Day, if we never danced all the rest of the year. Ah, how they danced at home there in the village! But now, it was not Easter at all, and yet the sun danced; what should it mean? And it came to Marie's mind that perhaps the Good Lord had told it to dance, for a sign to her that all would go well, and that she was doing quite right to run away from persons with the evil eye. When you came to think of it, what was more probable? They always said, those girls in the village, that the saints did the things they asked them to do. When Barbe lost her gold earring, did not Saint Joseph find it for her, and tell her to look among the potato-parings that had been thrown out the day before? and there, sure enough, it was, and the pigs never touching it, because they had been told not to touch! Well, and if the saints could do that, it would be a pity indeed if the Good Lord could not make the sun dance when he felt like doing a kind thing for a poor girl.

With the dazzle of that dancing sun still in her eyes, with happy thoughts filling her mind, Marie turned the corner of the straggling road that was called a street by the people who lived along it,—turned the corner, and almost fell into the arms of a man, who was coming in the opposite direction. Both uttered a cry at the same moment: Marie first giving a little startled shriek, but her voice dying away in terrified silence as she saw the man's face; the latter uttering a shout of delight, of fierce and cruel triumph, that rang out strangely in the quiet morning air. For this was Le Boss!

A man with a bloated, cruel face, sodden with drink and inflamed with all fierce and inhuman passions; a strong man, who held the trembling girl by the shoulder as if she were a reed, and gazed into her face with eyes of fiendish triumph; an angry man, who poured out a torrent of furious words, reproaching, threatening, by turns, as he found his victim once more within his grasp, just when he had given up all hope of finding her again. Ah, but he had her now, though! let her try it again, to run away! she would find even this time that she had enough, but another time—and on and on, as a coarse and brutal man can go on to a helpless creature that is wholly in his power.

Marie was silent, cowering in his grasp, looking about with hunted, despairing eyes. There was nothing to do, no word to say that would help. It had all been a mistake,—the sun dancing, the heavens bending down to aid and cheer her,—all had been a mistake, a lie. There was nothing now for the rest of her life but this,—this brutality that clutched and shook her slender figure, this hatred that hissed venomous words in her ear. This was the end, forever, till death should come to set her free.

But what was this? what was happening? For the hateful voice faltered, the grasp on her shoulder weakened, the blaze of the fierce eyes turned from her. A cry was heard, a wild, inarticulate cry of rage, of defiance; the next moment something rushed past her like a flash; there was a brief struggle, a shout, an oath, then a heavy fall. When the bewildered child could clear her eyes from the mist of fright that clouded them, Le Boss was lying on the ground; and towering over him like an avenging spirit, his blue eyes aflame, his strong hands clenched for another blow, stood Jacques De Arthenay.

Just what happened next, Marie never quite knew. Words were said as in a dream. Was it a real voice that was saying: "This is my wife, you dog! take yourself out of my sight, before worse comes to you!" Was it real? and did Le Boss, gathering himself up from the grass with foul curses, too horrible to think of—did he make reply that she was his property, that he had bought her, paid for her, and would have his own! And then the other voice again, saying, "I tell you she is my wife, the wife of a free man. Speak, Mary, and tell him you are my wife!" And did she—with those blue eyes on her, which she had never met before, but which now caught and chained her gaze, so that she could not look away, try as she might—did she of her own free will answer, "Yes, Monsieur, I am your wife, if you say it; if you will keep me from him, Monsieur!" Then—Marie did not know what came then. There were more words between the two men, loud and fierce on one side, low and fierce on the other; and then Le Boss was gone, and she was walking back to the house with the man who had saved her, the man to whom she belonged now; the strong man, whose hand, holding hers as they walked, trembled far more than her own. But Marie did not feel as if she should ever tremble again. For that one must be alive, must have strength in one's limbs; and was she dead, she wondered, or only asleep? and would she wake up some happy moment, and find herself in the little white bed at Abiroc's house, or better still, out in the blessed fields, alone with the birds under the free sky?

CHAPTER VI.

WEDLOCK.

They were married that very day. Abby begged piteously for a little delay, that she might make clothes, and give her pretty pet a "good send-off;" but De Arthenay would not hear of it. Mary was his wife in the sight of God; let her become so in the sight of man! So a white gown was found and put on the little passive creature, and good Abby, crying with excitement, twined some flowers in the soft dark hair, and thought that even Sister Lizzie, in her blue silk dress and chip bonnet, had not made so lovely a bride as this stranger, this wandering child from no one knew where. The wedding took place in Abby's parlor, with only Abby herself and a single neighbour for witnesses. A little crowd gathered round the door, however, to see how Jacques De Arthenay looked when he'd made a fool of himself, as they expressed it. They were in a merry mood, the friendly neighbours, and had sundry jests ready to crack upon the bridegroom when he should appear; but when he finally stood in the doorway, with the little pale bride on his arm, it became apparent that jests were not in order. People calc'lated that Jacques was in one of his moods, and was best not to be spoke with just that moment; besides, 't was no time for them to be l'iterin' round staring, with all there was to be done. So the crowd melted away, and only Abby followed the new-married couple to their own home. She, walking behind in much perturbation of spirit, noticed that on the threshold Marie stumbled, and seemed about to fall, and that Jacques lifted her in his arms as if she were a baby, and carried her into the room. He had not seemed to notice till that moment that the child was carrying her violin-case, though to be sure it was plain enough to see, but as he lifted her, it struck against the door-jamb, and he glanced down and saw it. When Abby came in (for this was to be her good-by to them, as she was to leave that afternoon for her sister's home), De Arthenay had the case in his hand, and was speaking in low, earnest tones.

"You cannot have this thing, Mary! It is a thing of evil, and may not be in a Christian household. You are going to leave all those things behind you now, and there must be nothing to recall that life with those bad people. I will burn the evil thing now, and it shall be a sweet savour to the Lord, even a marriage sacrifice." As he spoke he opened the case, and taking out the violin, laid it across his knee, intending to break it into pieces; but at this Marie broke out into a cry, so wild, so piercing, that he paused, and Abby ran to her and took her in, her arms, and pressed her to her kind breast, and comforted her as one comforts a little child. Then she turned to the stern-eyed bridegroom.

"Jacques," she pleaded, "don't do it! don't do such a thing on your wedding-day, if you have a heart in you. Don't you see how she feels it? Put the fiddle away, if you don't want it round; put it up garret, and let it lay there, till she's wonted a little to doing without it. Take it now out of her sight and your own, Jacques De Arthenay, or you'll be sorry for it when you have done a mischief you can't undo."

Abby wondered afterward what power had spoken in her voice; it must have had some unusual force, for De Arthenay, after a moment's hesitation, did as she bade him,—turned slowly and left the room, and the next moment was heard mounting the garret stairs. While he was gone, she still held Marie in her arms, and begged her not to tremble so, and told her that her husband was a good man, a kind man, that he had never hurt any one in his life except evil-doers, and had been a good son and a good brother to his own people while they lived. Then she bade the child look around at her new home, and see how neat and good everything was, and how tastefully Jacques had arranged it all for her. "Why, he vallies the ground you step on, child!" she cried. "You don't want to be afraid of him, dear. You can do anything you're a mind to with him, I tell you. See them flowers there, in the chaney bowl! Now he never looked at a flower in his life, Jacques didn't; but knowing you set by them, he went out and picked them pretty ones o' purpose. Now I call that real thoughtful, don't you, Maree?"

So the good soul talked on, soothing the girl, who said no word, only trembled, and gazed at her with wide, frightened eyes; but Abby's heart was heavy within her, and she hardly heard her own cheery words. What kind of union was this likely to be, with such a beginning! Why had she not realised, before it was too late, how set Jacques was in his ways, and how he never would give in to the heathen notions and fiddling ways of the foreign child?

Sadly the good woman bade farewell to the bridal couple, and left them alone in their new home. On the threshold she turned back for a moment, and had a moment's comfort; for Jacques had taken Marie's hands in his own, and was gazing at her with such love in his eyes that it must have melted a stone, Abby thought; and perhaps Marie thought so too, for she forgot to make the horns, and smiled back, a little faint piteous smile, into her husband's face.

31

So Abby went away to the West, to tend her sister, and Jacques and Marie De Arthenay began their life together.

It was not so very terrible, Marie found after a while. Of course a person could not always help it, to have the evil eye; it had happened that even the best of persons had it, and sometimes without knowing it. The Catholic girls at home in the village had a saint who always carried her eyes about in a plate because they were evil, and she was afraid of hurting some one with them. (Poor Saint Lucia! this is a new rendering of thy martyrdom!) Yes, indeed! Marie was no Catholic, but she had seen the picture, and knew that it was so. And oh, he did mean to be kind, her husband! that saw itself more and more plainly every day.

Then, there was great pleasure in the housekeeping. Marie was a born housewife, with delicate French hands, and an inborn skill in cookery, the discovery of which gave her great delight. Everything in the kitchen was fresh and clean and sweet, and in the garden were fruits, currants and blackberries and raspberries, and every kind of vegetable that grew in the village at home, with many more that were strange to her. She found never-ending pleasure in concocting new dishes, little triumphs of taste and daintiness, and trying them on her silent husband. Sometimes he did not notice them at all, but ate straight on, not knowing a delicate fricassee from a junk of salt beef; that was very trying. But again he would take notice, and smile at her with the rare sweet smile for which she was beginning to watch, and praise the prettiness and the flavor of what was set before him. But sometimes, too, dreadful things happened. One day Marie had tried her very best, and had produced a dish for supper of which she was justly proud,—a little *friture* of lamb, delicate golden-brown, with crimson beets and golden carrots, cut in flower-shapes, neatly ranged around. Such a pretty dish was never seen, she thought; and she had put it on the best platter, the blue platter with the cow and the strawberries on it; and when she set it before her husband, her dark eyes were actually shining with pleasure, and she was thinking that if he were very pleased, but very, very, she might possibly have courage to call him "Mon ami," which she had thought several times of doing. It had such a friendly sound, "Mon ami!"

But alas! when De Arthenay came to the table he was in one of his dark moods; and when his eyes fell on the festal dish, he started up, crying out that the devil was tempting him, and that he and his house should be lost through the wiles of the flesh; and so caught up the dish and flung it on the fire, and bade his trembling wife bring him a crust of dry bread. Poor Marie! she was too frightened to cry, though all her woman's soul was in arms at the destruction of good food, to say nothing of the wound to her house-wifely pride. She sat silent, eating nothing, only making believe, when her husband looked her way, to crumble a bit of bread. And when that wretched meal was over, Jacques called her to his side, and took out the great black Bible, and read three chapters of denunciation from Jeremiah, that made Marie's blood chill in her veins, and sent her shivering to her bed. The next day he would eat nothing but Indian meal porridge, and the next; and it was a week before Marie ventured to try any more experiments in cookery.

Marie had a great dread of the black Bible. She was sure it was a different Bible from the one which Mere Jeanne used to read at home, for that was full of lovely things, while this was terrible. Sometimes Jacques would call her to him and question her, and that was really too frightful for anything. Perhaps he had been reading aloud, as he was fond of doing in the evenings, some denunciatory passage from the psalms or the prophets. "Mary," he would say, turning to her, as she sat with her knitting in the corner, "what do you think of that passage?"

"I think him horreebl'," Marie would answer. "Why do you read of such things, Jacques! Why you not have the good Bible, as we have him in France, why?"

"There is but one Bible, Mary, but one in the world; and it is all good and beautiful, only our sinful eyes cannot always see the glory of it."

"Ah, but no!" Marie would persist, shaking her head gravely. "Mere Jeanne's Bible was all ozer, so I tell you. Not black and horreebl', no! but red, all red, wiz gold on him, and in his side pictures, all bright and preetty, and good words, good ones, what make the good feel in my side. Yes, that is the Bible I have liked."

"Mary, I tell you it was no Bible, unless it was this very one. They bind it in any colour they like, don't you see, child? It isn't the cover that makes the book. I fear you weren't brought up a Christian, Mary. It is a terrible thing to think of, my poor little wife. You must let me teach you; you must talk with Elder Beach on Sunday afternoons. Assuredly he will help you, if I am found unworthy."

But Marie would have none of this. She was a Christian, she maintained as stoutly as her great fear of her husband would permit. She had been baptized, and taught all that one should be taught. But it was all different. Her Bible told that we must love people, but love everybody, always, all times; and this black book said that we must kill them with swords, and dash them against stones, and pray bad things to happen to them. It stood to reason that it was not the same Bible, *hein*? At this Jacques De Arthenay started, and took himself by the hair with both hands, as he did when something moved him strongly. "Those were bad people, Mary!" he cried. "Don't you see? they withstood the Elect, and they were slain. And we must think about these things, and think of our sins, and the sins of others as a warning to ourselves. Sin is awful, black, horrible! and its wages is death,—death, do you hear?"

When he cried out in this way, like a wild creature, Marie did not dare to speak again; but she would murmur under her breath in French, as she bent lower over her knitting, "Nevertheless, Mere Jeanne's good Lord was good, and yours—"; and then she would quietly turn a hairpin upside down in her hair, for it was quite certain that if she caught Jacques's eye when he was in this mood, her hand would wither, or her hair fall out, or at the very least the cream all sour in the pans; and when one's hands were righteously busy, as with knitting, one might make the horns with other things, and a hairpin was very useful. She wished she had a little coral hand, such as she had once seen at a fair, with the fingers making the horns in the proper manner; it would be a great convenience, she thought with a sigh.

But he was always sorry after these dark times; and when he sat and held her hand, as he did sometimes, silent for the most part, but gazing at her with eyes of absolute, unspeakable love, Marie was pleased, almost content: as nearly content as one could be with the half of one's life taken away.

CHAPTER VII.

LOOKING BACK.

The half of a life! for so Marie counted the loss of her violin. She never spoke of this—to whom should she speak? In her husband's eyes it was a thing accursed, she knew. She almost hoped he had forgotten about the precious treasure that lay so quietly in some dark nook in the lonely garret; for as long as he did not think of it, it was safe there, and she should not feel that terrible anguish that had seemed to rend body and soul when she saw him lay the violin across his knee to break it. And Abby came not, and gave no sign; and there was no one else.

She saw little of the neighbours at first. The women looked rather askance at her, and thought her little better than a fool, even if she had contrived to make one of Jacques De Arthenay. She never seemed to understand their talk, and had a way of looking past them, as if unaware of their presence, that was disconcerting, when one thought well of oneself. But Marie was not a fool, only a child; and she did not look at the women simply because she was not thinking of them. With the children, however, it was different Marie felt that she would have a great deal to say to the children, if only she had the half of her that could talk to them. Ah, how she would speak, with Madame on her arm! What wonders she could tell them, of fairies and witches, of flowers that sang and birds that danced! But this other part of her was shy, and she did not feel that she had anything worth saying to the little ones, who looked at her with half-frightened, half-inviting eyes when they passed her door. By-and-by, however, she mustered up courage, and called one or two of them to her, and gave them flowers from her little garden. Also a pot of jam with a spoon in it proved an eloquent argument in favour of friendship; and after a while the children fell into a way of sauntering past with backward glances, and were always glad to come in when Marie knocked on the window, or came smiling to the door, with her handkerchief tied under her chin and her knitting in her hand. It was only when her husband was away that this happened; Marie would not for worlds have called a child to meet her husband's eyes, those blue eyes of which, she stood in such terror, even when she grew to love them.

One little boy in particular came often, when the first shyness had worn away. He was an orphan, like Marie herself: a pretty, dark-eyed little fellow, who looked, she fancied, like the children at home in France. He did not expect her to talk and answer questions, but was content to sit, as she loved to do, gazing at the trees or the clouds that went sailing by, only now and then uttering a few quiet words that seemed in harmony with the stillness all around. I have said that Jacques De Arthenay's house lay somewhat apart from the village street. It was a pleasant house, long and low, painted white, with vines trained over the lower part. Directly opposite was a pine grove, and here Marie and her little friend loved to sit, listening to the murmur of the wind in the dark feathery branches. It was the sound of the sea, Marie told little Petie. As to how it got there, that was another matter; but it was undoubtedly the sound of the sea, for she had been at sea, and recognised it at once.

"What does it say?" asked the child one day.

"Of words," said Marie, "I hear not any, Petie. But it wants always somesing, do you hear? It is hongry always, and makes moans for the sorry thinks it has in its heart."

"I am hungry in my stomach, not in my heart," objected Petie.

But Marie nodded her head sagely. "Yes," she said. "It is that you know not the deeference, Petie, bit-ween those. To be hongry at the stomach, that is made better when you eat cakes, do you see, or _pot_atoes. But when the heart is hongry, then—ah, yes, that is ozer thing." And she nodded again, and glanced up at the attic window, and sighed.

It was a long time before she spoke of her past life; but when she found that Petie had no sharp-eyed mother at home, only a deaf great-aunt who asked no questions, she began to give him little glimpses of the circus world, which filled him with awe and rapture. It was hardly a real circus, only a little strolling *troupe*, with some performing dogs, and a few trained horses and ponies, and two tight-rope dancers; then there were two other musicians, and Marie herself, besides Le Boss and his family, and Old Billy, who took care of the horses and did the dirty work. It was about the dogs that Petie liked best to hear; of the wonderful feats of Monsieur George, the great brindled greyhound, and the astonishing sagacity of Coquelicot, the poodle.

"Monsieur George, he could jump over anything, yes! He was always jump, jump, all day long, to practise himself. Over our heads all, that was nothing, yet he did it always when we come in the tent, *pour saluer*, to say the how you do. But one day come in a man to see Le Boss, very tall, oh, like mountains, and on him a tall hat. And Monsieur George, he not stopped to measure with his eye, for fear he be too late with the *politesse*, and he jump, and carry away the man's hat, and knock him down and come plomp, down on him. Yes, very funny! The man got a bottle in his hat, and that break, and run all over him, and he say, oh, he say all things what you think of. But Monsieur George was so 'shamed, he go away and hide, and not for a week we see him again. Le Boss think that man poison him, and he goes to beat him; but that same day Monsieur George come back, and stop outside the tent and call us all to come out. And when we come, he run back, and say, 'Look here, what I do!' and he jump, and go clean over the tent, and not touch him wiz his foot. Yes, I saw it: very fine dog, Monsieur George! But Coquelicot, he have more thinking than Monsieur George. He very claiver, Coquelicot! Some of zem think him a witch, but I think not that. He have minds, that was all. But his legs so short, and that make him hate Monsieur George."

"My legs are short," objected Petie, stretching out a pair of plump calves, "but that doesn't make me hate people."

"Ah, but if you see a little boy what can walk over the roof of the house, you want the same to do it, *n'est-ce-pas*?" cried Marie. "You try, and try, and when you cannot jump, you think that not a so nize little boy as when his legs were short. So boy, so dog. Coquelicot, all his life he want to jump like Monsieur George, and all his life he cannot jump at all. You say to him, 'Coquelicot, are you foolishness? you can do feefty things and George not one of zem: you can read the letters, and find the things in the pocket, and play the ins_tru_ment, and sing the tune to make die people of laughing, yet you are not _con_tent. Let him have in peace his legs, Monsieur George, then!' But no! and every time Monsieur George come down from the great jump, Coquelicot is ready, and bite his legs so hard what he can."

Petie laughed outright. "I think that's awful funny!" he said. "I say, Mis' De Arthenay, I'd like to seen him bite his legs. Did he holler?"

"Monsieur George? He cry, and go to his bed. All the dogs, they afraid of Coquelicot, because he have the minds. And he, Coquelicot, he fear nossing, except Madame when she is angry."

"Who was she?" asked Petie,—"a big dog?"

"Ah, dog, no!" cried Marie, her face flushing. "Madame my violon, my life, my pleasure, my friend. Ah, *mon Dieu*, what friend have I?" Her breast heaved, and she broke into a wild fit of crying, forgetting the child by her side, forgetting everything in the world save the hunger at her heart for the one creature to whom she could speak, and who could speak in turn to her.

Petie sat silent, frightened at the sudden storm of sobs and tears. What had he done, he wondered? At length he mustered courage to touch his friend's arm softly with his little hand.

"I didn't go to do it!" he said. "Don't ye cry, Mis' De Arthenay! I don't know what I did, but I didn't go to do it, nohow."

Marie turned and looked at him, and smiled through her tears. "Dear little Petie!" she said, stroking the curly head, "you done nossing, little Petie. It was the honger, no more! Oh, no more!" she caught her breath, but choked the sob back bravely, and smiled again. Something woke in her child heart, and bade her not sadden the heart of the younger child with a grief which was not his. It is one of the lessons of life, and it was well with Marie that she learned it early.

"Madame, my violon," she resumed after a pause, speaking cheerfully, and wiping her eyes with her apron, "she have many voices, Petie; tousand voices, like all birds, all winds, all song in the world; and she have an angry voice, too, deep down, what make you tr-remble in your heart, if you are bad. *Bien!* Sometime Coquelicot, he been bad, very bad. He know so much, that make him able for the bad, see, like for the good. Yes! Sometime, he steal the sugar; sometime he come in when we make music, and make wiz us yells, and spoil the music; sometime he make the horreebl' faces at the poppies and make scream them with fear."

"Kin poppies scream?" asked Petie, opening great eyes of wonder. "My! ourn can't. We've got big red ones, biggest ever you see, but I never heerd a sound out of 'em."

Explanations ensued, and a digression in favour of the six puppies, whose noses were softer and whose tails were funnier than anything else in the known, world; and then—

"So Coquelicot, he come and he sit down before the poppies, and he open his mouth, so!" here Marie opened her pretty mouth, and tried to look like a malicious poodle,—with singular lack of success; but Petie was delighted, and clapped his hands and laughed.

"And then," Marie went on, "Lisette, she is the poppies' mother, and she hear them, and she come wiz yells, too, and try to drive Coquelicot, but he take her wiz his teeth and shake her, and throw her away, and go on to make faces, and all is horreebl' noise, to wake deads. So Old Billy call me, and I come, and I go softly behind Coquelicot, and down I put me, and Madame speak in her angry voice justly in Coquelicot's ear. 'La la! tra la li la!' deep down like so, full wiz angryness, terreebl', yes! And Coquelicot he jump, oh my! oh my! never he could jump so of all his life. And the tail bit-ween his legs, and there that he run, run, as if all devils run after him. Yes, funny, Petie, vairy funny!" She laughed, and Petie laughed in violent, noisy peals, as children love to do, each gust of merriment fanning the fire for another, till all control is lost, and the little one drops into an irrepressible fit of the "giggles." So they sat under the pine-trees, the two children, and laughed, and Marie forgot the hunger at her heart; till suddenly she looked and saw her husband standing near, leaning on his rake and gazing at her with grave, uncomprehending eyes. Then the laugh froze on her lips, and she rose hastily, with the little timid smile which was all she had for Jacques (yet he was hungry too, so hungry! and knew not what ailed him!) and went to meet him; while Petie ran away through the grove, as fast as his little legs would carry him.

CHAPTER VIII.

A FLOWER IN THE SNOW.

The winter, when it came, was hard for Marie. She had never known severe weather before, and this season it was bitter cold. People shook their heads, and said that old times had come again, and no mistake. There was eager pride in the lowest mercury, and the man whose thermometer registered thirty degrees below zero was happier than he who could boast but of twenty-five. There was not so much snow as in milder seasons, but the cold held without breaking, week after week: clear weather; no wind, but the air taking the breath from the dryness of it, and in the evening the haze hanging blue and low that tells of intensest cold. As the snow fell, it remained. The drifts and hollows never changed their shape, as in a soft or a windy season, but seemed fixed as they were for all time. Across the road from Jacques De Arthenay's house, a huge drift had been piled by the first snowstorm of the winter. Nearly as high as the house it was, and its top combed forward, like a wave ready to break; and in the blue hollow beneath the curling crest was the likeness of a great face. A rock cropped out, and ice had formed upon its surface, so that the snow fell away from it. The explanation was simple enough; Jacques De Arthenay, coming and going at his work, never so much as looked at it; but to Marie it was a strange and a dreadful thing to see. Night and morning, in the cold blue light of the winter moon and the bright hard glitter of the winter sun, the face was always there, gazing in at her through the window, seeing everything she did, perhaps—who could tell?—seeing everything she thought. She changed her seat, and drew down the blind that faced the drift; yet it had a strange fascination for her none the less, and many times in the day she would go and peep through the blind, and shiver, and then come away moaning in a little way that she had when she was alone. It was pitiful to see how she shrank from the cold,—the tender creature who seemed born to live and bloom with the flowers, perhaps to wither with them. Sometimes it seemed to her as if she could not bear it, as if she must run away and find the birds, and the green and joyous things that she loved. The pines were always green, it is true, in the little grove across the way; but it was a solemn and gloomy green, to her child's mind,—she had not yet learned to love the steadfast pines. Sometimes she would open the door with a wild thought of flying out, of flying far away, as the birds did, and rejoining them in southern countries where the sun was warm, and not a fire that froze while it lighted one. So cold! so cold! But when she stood thus, the little wild heart beating fiercely in her, the icy blast would come and chill her into quiet again, and turn the blood thick, so that it ran slower in her veins; and she would think of the leagues and leagues of pitiless snow and ice that lay between her and the birds, and would close the door again, and go back to her work with that little weary moan.

Her husband was very kind in these days; oh, very kind and gentle. He kept the dark moods to himself, if they came upon him, and tried even to be gay, though he did not know how to set about it. If he had ever known or looked at a child, this poor man, he would have done better; but it was not a thing that he had ever thought of, and he did not yet know that Marie was a child. Sometimes when she saw him looking at her with the grave, loving, uncomprehending look that so often followed her as she moved about, she would come to him and lay her head against his shoulder, and remain quiet so for many minutes; but when he moved to stroke her dark head, and say, "What is it, Mary? what troubles you?" she could only say that it was cold, very cold, and then go away again about her work.

Sometimes an anguish would seize him, when he saw how pale and thin she grew, and he would send for the village doctor, and beg him to give her some "stuff" that would make her plump and rosy again; but the good man shook his head, and said she needed nothing, only care and kindness,—kindness, he repeated, with some emphasis, after a glance at De Arthenay's face, and good food. "Cheerfulness," he said, buttoning up his fur coat under his chin,— "cheerfulness, Mr. De Arthenay, and plenty of good things to eat. That's all she needs." And he went away wondering whether the little creature would pull through the winter or not.

And Jacques did not throw the food into the fire any more; he even tried to think about it, and care about it. And he got out the Farmer's Almanac,—yes, he did,—and tried reading the jokes aloud, to see if they would amuse Mary; but they did not amuse her in the least, or him either, so that was given up. And so the winter wore on.

It had to end sometime; even that winter could not last forever. The iron grasp relaxed: fitfully at first, with grim clutches and snatches at its prey, gripping it the closer because it knew the time was near when all power would go, drop off like a garment, melt away like a stream. The unchanging snow-forms began to shift, the keen outlines wavered, grew indistinct, fell into ruin, as the sun grew warm again, and sent down rays that were no longer like lances of diamond. The glittering face in the hollow of the great drift lost its watchful look, softened, grew dim and blurred; one morning it was gone. That day Marie sang a little song, the first she had sung through all the long, cruel season. She drew up the blind and gazed out; she wrapped a shawl round her head and went and stood at the door, afraid of nothing now, not even thinking of making those tiresome horns. She was aware of something new in the air she breathed. It was still cold, but with a difference; there was a breathing as of life, where all had been dry, cold death. There was a sense of awakening everywhere; whispers seemed to come and go in the tops of the pine-trees, telling of coming things, of songs that would be sung in their branches, as they had been sung before; of blossoms that would spring at their feet, brightening the world with gold and white and crimson.

Life! life stirring and waking everywhere, in sky and earth; soft clouds sweeping across the blue, softening its cold brightness, dropping rain as they go; sap creeping through the ice-bound stems, slowly at first, then running freely, bidding the tree awake and be at its work, push out the velvet pouch that holds the yellow catkin, swell and polish the pointed leaf-buds: life working silently under the ground, brown seeds opening their leaves to make way for the tender shoot that shall draw nourishment from them and push its way on and up while they die content, their work being done; roots creeping here and there, threading their way through the earth, softening, loosening, sucking up moisture and sending it aloft to carry on the great work,—life everywhere, pulsing in silent throbs, the heart-beats of Nature; till at last the time is ripe, the miracle is prepared, and

> "In green underwood and cover
> Blossom by blossom the spring begins."

Marie too, the child-woman, standing in her doorway, felt the thrill of new life; heard whispers of joy, but knew not what they meant; saw a radiance in the air that was not all sunlight; was conscious of a warmth at her heart which she had never known in her merriest days. What did it all mean? Nay, she could not tell, she was not yet awake. She thought of her friend, of the silent voice that had spoken so often and so sweetly to her, and the desire grew strong upon her. If she died for it, she must play once more on her violin.

There came a day in spring when the desire mastered the fear that was in her. It was a perfect afternoon, the air a-lilt with bird-songs, and full of the perfume of early flowers. Her husband was ploughing in a distant field, and surely would not return for an hour or two; what might one not do in an hour? She called her little friend, Petie, who was hovering about the door, watching for her. Quickly, with fluttering breath, she told him what she meant to do, bade him be brave and fear nothing; locked the door, drew down the blinds, and closed the heavy wooden shutters; turned to the four corners of the room, bowing to each corner, as she muttered some words under her breath; and then, catching the child's hand in hers, began swiftly and lightly to mount the attic stairs.

CHAPTER X.

DE AKTHENAY'S VIGIL.

Was it a *loup-garou* in the attic? was it a *loup-garou* that drew that long, sighing breath, as of a soul in pain; was it a *loup-garou* that now groped its way to the other staircase, that which led up from the woodshed, pausing now and then, and going blindly, and breathing still heavily and slow?

De Arthenay had come up to the attic in search of something, tools, maybe, or seeds, or the like, for many odd things were stowed away under the over-hanging rafters. He heard steps, and stood still, knowing that it must be his wife who was coming up, and thinking to have pleasure just by watching her as she went on some little household errand, such as brought himself. She would know nothing of his presence, and so she would be free, unrestrained by any shyness or—or fear; if it was fear. So he had stood in his dark corner, and had seen little, indeed, but heard all; and it was a wild and a miserable man that crept down the narrow stairway and out into the fresh air.

He did not know where he was going. He wandered on and on, hearing always that sound in his ears, the soft, sweet tones of the accursed instrument that was wiling his wife, his own, his beloved, to her destruction. The child, too, how would it be for him? But the child was a smaller matter. Perhaps,—who knows? a child can live down sin. But Mary, whom he fancied saved, cured, the evil thing rooted out of her heart and remembrance!

Mary; Mary! He kept saying her name over and over to himself, sometimes aloud, in a passion of reproach, sometimes softly, broodingly, with love and pathos unutterable. What power there was in that wicked voice! He had never rightly heard it before, never, save that instant when she stood playing in the village street, and he saw her for a moment and loved her forever. Oh, he had heard, to be sure, this or that strolling fiddler,—godless, tippling wretches, who rarely came to the village, and never set foot there twice, he thought with pride. But this, this was different! What power! what sweetness, filling his heart with rapture even while his spirit cried out against it! What voices, entreating, commanding, uplifting!

Nay, what was he saying? and who did not know that Satan could put on an angel's look when it pleased him? and if a look, why not a voice? When had a fiddle played godly tunes, chant or psalm? when did it do aught else but tempt the foolish to their folly, the wicked to their iniquity?

Mary! Mary! How lovely she was, in the faint gleams of light that fell about her, there in the dim old attic! He felt her beauty, almost, more than he saw it. And all this year, while he had thought her growing in grace, silently, indeed, but he hoped truly, she had been hankering for the forbidden thing, had been planning deceit in her heart, and had led away the innocent child to follow unrighteousness with her. He would go back, and do what he should have done a year ago,—what he would have done, had he not yielded to the foolish talk of a foolish woman. He would go back, and burn the fiddle, and silence forever that sweet, insidious music, with its wicked murmurs that stole into a man's heart—even a man's, and one who knew the evil, and abhorred it. The smoke of it once gone up to heaven, there would be an end. He should have his wife again, his own, and nothing should come between them more. Yes, he would go back, in a little while, as soon as those sounds had died away from his ears. What was the song she sung there?

> "'Tis long and long I have loved thee!
> I'll ne'er forget thee more."

She would forget it, though, surely, surely, when it was gone, breathed out in flame and ashes: when he could say to her, "There is no more any such thing in my house and yours, Mary, Mary."

How tenderly he would tell her, though! It would hurt, yes! but not so much as her look would hurt him when he told her. Ah, she loved the wooden thing best! He was dumb, and it spoke to her in a thousand tones! Even he had understood some of them. There was one note that was like his mother's voice when she lifted it up in the hymn she loved best,—his gentle mother, dead so long, so long ago. She—why, she loved music; he had forgotten that. But only psalms, only godly hymns, never anything else.

What devil whispered in his ear, "She never heard anything else. She would have loved this too, this too, if she had had the chance, if she had heard Mary play!" He put his hands to his ears, and almost ran on. Where was he going? He did not ask, did not think. He only knew that it was a relief to be walking, to get farther and farther away from what he loved and fain would cherish, from what he hated and would fain destroy.

The grass grew long and rank under his feet; he stumbled, and paused for a moment, out of breath, to look about him. He was in the old burying-ground, the grey stones rearing their heads to peer at him as he hurried on. Ah, there was one stone here that belonged to him. He had not been in the place since he was a child; he cared nothing about the dead of long ago: but now the memory of it all came back upon him, and he sought and found the grey sunken stone, and pulled away the grass from it, and read the legend with eyes that scarcely saw what they looked at.

"D'Arthenay, tenez foi!"

And the place was free from moss, as they always said; the rude scratch, as of a sharp-pointed instrument. Did it mean anything? He dropped beside it for a minute, and studied the stone; then rose and went his way again, still wandering on and on, he knew not whither.

Darkness came, and he was in the woods, stumbling here and there, driven as by a strong wind, scorched as by a flame. At last he sank down at the foot of a great oak-tree, in a place he knew well, even in the dark: he could go no farther.

"D'Arthenay, tenez foi!"

It whispered in his ears, and seemed for a little to drown the haunting notes of the violin. He, the Calvinist, the practical man, who believed in two things outside the visible world, a great hell and a small heaven, now felt spirits about him, saw visions that were not of this life. His ancestor, the Huguenot, stood before him, in cloak and band; in one hand a Bible, in the other a drawn dagger. His dark eyes pierced like a sword-thrust; his lips moved; and though no sound came, Jacques knew the words they framed.

"Tenez foi! Keep the faith that I brought across the sea, leaving for it fair fields and vineyards, castle and tower and town. Keep the faith for which I bled, for which I died here in the wilderness, leaving only these barren acres, and the stone that bears my last word, my message to those who should come after me. Keep the faith for which my fair wife faded and died, far away from home and friends! Let no piping or jigging or profane sound be in thy house, but let it be the house of fasting and of prayer, even as my house was. Keep faith! If thy right hand offend thee, cut it off and cast it from thee!"

Who else was there,—what gentle, pallid ghost, with sad, faint eyes? The face was dim and shadowy, for he had been a little child when his mother died. She was speaking too, but what were these words she was saying? "Keep faith, my son! ay! but keep it with your wife too, the child you wedded whether she would or no, and from whom you are taking the joy of childhood, the light of youth. Keep faith as the sun keeps it, as the summer keeps it, not as winter and the night."

What did that mean? keep faith with her, with his wife? how else should he do it but by saving her from the wrath to come, by plucking her as a flower out of the mire?

"What shall I save but her soul, yea, though her body perish?"

He spoke out in his trouble, and the vision seemed to shrink and waver under his gaze; but the faint voice sighed again,—or was it only the wind in the pine-trees?—"Care thou for her earthly life, her earthly joy, for God is mindful of her soul."

But then the deeper note struck in again,—or was it only a stronger gust, that bowed the branches, and murmured through all the airy depths above him?

"Keep the faith! Thou art a man, and wilt thou be drawn away by women, of whom the best are a stumbling-block and a snare for the feet? Destroy the evil thing! root it out from thy house! What are joys of this world, that we should think of them? Do they not lead to destruction, even the flowery path of it, going down to the mouth of the pit, and with no way leading thence? Who is the woman for whose sake thou wilt lose thine own soul? If thy right eye offend thee, pluck it out!"

So the night went on, and the voices, or the wind, or his own soul, cried, and answered, and cried again: and no peace came.

The night passed. As it drew to a close, all sound, all motion, died away; the darkness folded him close, like a mantle; the silence pressed upon him like hands that held him down. Like a log the man lay at the foot of the great tree, and his soul lay dead within him.

At last a change came; or did he sleep, and dream of a change? A faint trembling in the air, a faint rustling that lost itself almost before it reached the ear. It was gone, and all was still once more; yet with a difference. The darkness lay less heavily: one felt that it hid many things, instead of filling the world with itself alone.

Hark! the murmur again, not lost this time, but coming and going, lightly, softly, brushing here and there, soft dark wings fanning the air, making it ever lighter, thinner. Gradually the veil lifted; things stood out, black against black, then black against grey; straight majesty of tree-trunks, bending lines of bough and spray, tender grace of ferns.

And now, what is this? A sound from the trees themselves,—no multitudinous murmur this time, but a single note, small and clear and sweet, breaking like a golden arrow of sound through the cloudy depths.

Chirp, twitter! and again from the next tree, and the next, and now from all the trees, short triads, broken snatches, and at last the full chorus of song, choir answering to choir, the morning hymn of the forest.

Now, in the very tree beneath which the man lay, Chrysostom, the thrush, took up his parable, and preached his morning sermon; and if it had been set to words, they might have been something like these:—

"Sing! sing, brothers, sisters, little tender ones in the nest! Sing, for the morning is come, and God has made us another day. Sing! for praise is sweet, and our sweetest notes must show it forth. Song is the voice that God has given us to tell forth His goodness, to speak gladly of the wondrous things He hath made. Sing, brothers and sisters! be joyful, be joyful in the Lord! all sorrow and darkness is gone away, away, and light is here, and morning, and the world wakes with us to gladness and the new day. Sing, and let your songs be all of joy, joy, lest there be in the wood any sorrowing creature, who might go sadly through the day for want of a voice of cheer, to tell him that God is love, is love. Wake from thy dream, sad heart, if the friendly wood hold such an one! Sorrow is night, and night is good, for rest, and for seeing of many stars, and for coolness and sweet odours; but now awake, awake, for the day is here, and the sun arises in his might,—the sun, whose name is joy, is joy, and, whose voice is praise. Sing, sing, and praise the Lord!"

So the bird sang, praising God, and the other birds, from tree and shrub, answered as best they might, each with his song of praise; and the man, lying motionless beneath the great tree, heard, and listened, and understood.

Still he lay there, with wide open eyes, while the golden morning broke over him, and the light came sifting down, through the leaves, checkering all the ground with gold. The wood now glowed with colour, russet and green and brown, wine-like red of the tree-trunks where the sun struck aslant on them, soft yellow greens where the young ferns uncurled their downy heads. The air was sweet, sweet, with the smell of morning; was the whole world new since last night?

Suddenly from the road near by (for he had gone round in a circle, and the wooded hollow where he lay was out of sight but not out of hearing of the country road which skirted the woods for many miles), from the road near by came the sound of voices,—men's voices, which fell strange and harsh on his ears, open for the first time to the music of the world, and still ringing with the morning hymn of joy. What were these harsh voices saying?

"They think she'll live now?"

"Yes, she'll pull through, unless she frets herself bad again about Jacques. Nobody'd heerd a word of him when I come away."

"Been out all night, has he?"

"Yes! went away without saying anything to her or anybody, far as I can make out. Been gone since yesterday afternoon, and some say—" The voices died away, and then the footsteps, and silence fell once more.

CHAPTER XI.

VITA NUOVA.

De Arthenay never knew how he reached home that day. The spot where he had been lying was several miles from the white cottage, yet he was conscious of no time, no distance. It seemed one burning moment, a moment never to be forgotten while he lived, till he found himself at the foot of the outer stairway, the stair that led to the attic. She might still be living, and he would not go to her without the thing she craved, the thing which could speak to her in the voice she understood.

Again a moment of half-consciousness, and he was standing in the doorway of her bedroom, looking in with blind eyes of dread. What should he see? what still form might break the outline of that white bed which she always kept so smooth and trim?

The silence cried out to him with a thousand voices, threatening, condemning, blasting; but the next moment it was broken.

"Mon ami!" said Marie. The words were faint, but there was a tone in them that had never been there before. "Jacques, mon ami, you are here! You did not go to leave me?"

The mist cleared from the man's eyes. He did not see Abby Rock, sitting by the bed, crying with joyful indignation; if he had seen her, it would not have been in the least strange for her to be there. He saw nothing—the world held nothing—but the face that looked at him from the pillow, the pale face, all soft and worn, yet full of light, full—was it true, or was he dreaming in the wood?—of love, of joy.

"Come in, Jacques!" said Abby, wondering at the look of the man. "Don't make a noise, but come in and sit down!"

De Arthenay did not move, but held out the violin in both hands with a strange gesture of submission.

"I have brought it, Mary!" he said. "You shall always have it now. I—I have learned a little—I know a little, now, of what it means. I hadn't understanding before, Mary. I meant no unkindness to you."

Abby laughed softly. "Jacques De Arthenay, come here!" she said. "What do you suppose Maree's thinking of fiddles now? Come here, man alive, and see your boy!"

But Marie laid one hand softly on the violin, as it lay on the bed beside her,— the hand that was not patting the baby; then she laid it, still softly, shyly, on her husband's head as he knelt beside her. "Jacques, mon ami," she whispered, "you are good! I too have learned. I was a child always, I knew nothing. See now, I love always Madame, my friend, and she is mine; but this, this is yours too, and mine too, our life, our own. Jacques, now we both know, and God, He tell us! See, the same God, only we did not know the first times. Now, always we know, and not forget! not forget!"

The baby woke and stirred. The tiny hand was outstretched and touched its father's hand, and a thrill ran through him from head to foot, softening the hard grain, melting, changing the fibre of his being. The husk that in those lonely hours in the forest had been loosened, broken, now fell away from him, and a new man knelt by the white bed, silent, gazing from child to wife with eyes more eloquent than any words could be. The baby's hand rested in his, and Marie laid her own over it; and Abby Rock rose and went away, closing the door softly after her.

THE END